Mom Likes Hats

by Michèle Dufresne

PIONEER VALLEY EDUCATIONAL PRESS, INC.

Mom likes the purple hat.

3

Mom likes the red hat.

5

Mom likes the white hat.

Mom likes the green hat.

9

Mom likes the yellow hat.

11

Mom likes the black hat.

Mom likes the pink hat.

Mom **loves**
the flowered hat.